© 1992 The Walt Disney Company

No portion of this book may be reproduced
without the written consent of The Walt Disney Company.

Produced by Kroha Associates, Inc.
Middletown, Connecticut

Illustrated by Yakovetic Productions

Written by M.C. Varley

Printed in the United States of America.

ISBN 1-56326-165-0

Detective Sebastian

"It has to be here somewhere!" the Little Mermaid exclaimed. She had searched every nook and cranny in her undersea grotto, but she still couldn't find what she was looking for.

"What's going on here?" complained Sebastian the crab. All the noise Ariel was making had awakened him from his afternoon nap.

"My favorite ring is missing!" Ariel explained. "I had it with me while I was making a sand sculpture of everyone at the beach. And now I can't find it anywhere!"

"Oh, no!" the Little Mermaid cried. "Do you think someone took my ring while I was making the sculpture?"

"But who would do such a thing?" gasped Sebastian.

"I don't know," Ariel replied. "But how else could it have disappeared? Oh, Sebastian, you've got to help me get my ring back!"

"Have no fear," replied Sebastian as he took a magnifying glass off Ariel's shelf and peered through it. "I'm a very good detective. *I'll* solve the mystery for you!"

Sebastian went to tell everyone to come to the lagoon later that afternoon for a very important meeting. First he told Flounder and Sandy, who were very curious about what was going on. "You'll just have to wait until the meeting to find out," replied Sebastian as he swam off to find Scales the dragon and Scuttle the seagull.

"Sounds very mysterious to me," Scales said when Sebastian told him and Scuttle about the big meeting.

"That's exactly right!" replied the crab. "It *is* a mystery!"

When everyone had gathered at the lagoon, Sebastian climbed to the top of the rock next to the Little Mermaid's sculpture and said, "Ariel's favorite ring has been missing since yesterday, when she made this sculpture. Since you were all here when the ring disappeared, I want to know everything you remember."

Flounder, Scales, Scuttle, and Sandy all looked at each other. Could one of them have taken the ring?

"We all know how much Scuttle likes little trinkets," said Flounder. "Come to think of it, I do remember him leaning on that rock yesterday."

"Me!" squawked the flustered bird. "What about Sandy? She's always talking about how beautiful Ariel's jewelry is!"

"That's silly!" said Sandy. "Fish don't wear rings! And besides, I think I saw Scales bring Ariel's ring into his cave!"

"What would I want with Ariel's ring?" the dragon replied. "My fingers are too big for a tiny ring like Ariel's!"

"That's right!" agreed Scuttle. "And I like *giving* Ariel trinkets and things — not *taking* them from her!"

"All right, everyone," Sebastian said, "instead of blaming each other, separate into pairs and look for clues."

So Scales and Scuttle went off to investigate the island.

Flounder and Sandy searched every inch of the ocean floor. There wasn't a clue anywhere.

"This is terrible!" Sandy said when she and Flounder arrived back at the lagoon. "If we don't find Ariel's ring, we'll always wonder if one of us took it."

"Ariel," Sebastian said, "tell us again what you remember from that morning. You must be leaving something out."

"Well, let's see," said Ariel, thinking hard. "Everyone was posing—except for you, Sebastian. I took off my ring and put it on this rock so it wouldn't get dirty, and then I finished making the sculpture. That night I noticed that I didn't have my ring. I went back to the rock to get it, but it was gone!"

"Hmmm, I don't have a clue," Sebastian said, leaning against the sculpture. But as he did, it started to crumble. "What are you doing?" the Little Mermaid cried. "Be careful!"

It was too late. A piece of the sculpture broke off and smashed on the ground.

"Look!" said Scuttle. "What's that?"

Something in the sand was sparkling in the sunlight.

"My ring!" the Little Mermaid squealed with delight. "It was inside the sculpture the whole time! I must have accidentally knocked it off the rock while I was making the sculpture!"

"Of course!" said Sebastian, even though he was just as surprised as everyone else. "I told you I would solve the mystery!"

"I'm sorry I thought one of you took my ring," Ariel said. "I hope I didn't hurt your feelings."

"I guess we should know better than to think one of us could have taken it," said Scales. "Friends should trust each other."

"How about posing for another sculpture?" the Little Mermaid asked her friends. "Sebastian, since you're the detective who solved the mystery, you stand in front."

"On one condition," said Sebastian as he slipped the ring on a piece of seaweed. "This time, wear the ring around your neck. We've had enough mysteries for one day!"